My SAD

A Crabtree Roots Book

AMY CULLIFORD

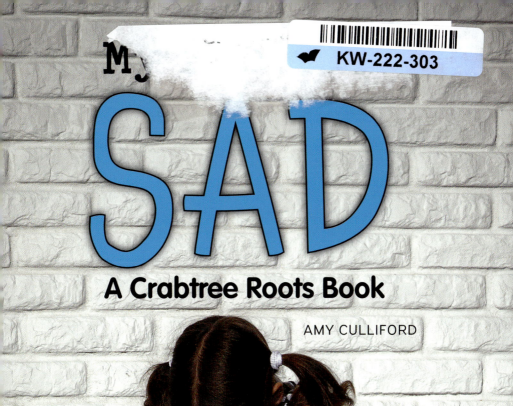

CRABTREE
Publishing Company
www.crabtreebooks.com

School-to-Home Support for Caregivers and Teachers

This book helps children grow by letting them practice reading. Here are a few guiding questions to help the reader with building his or her comprehension skills. Possible answers appear here in red.

Before Reading:
• What do I think this book is about?
  • *This book is about feeling sad.*
  • *This book is about what feeling sad looks like.*

• What do I want to learn about this topic?
  • *I want to learn what makes me feel sad.*
  • *I want to learn what feeling sad looks like.*

During Reading:
• I wonder why...
  • *I wonder why we frown when we are sad.*
  • *I wonder why we cry.*

• What have I learned so far?
  • *I have learned what feeling sad looks like.*
  • *I have learned that people cry when they are sad.*

After Reading:
• What details did I learn about this topic?
  • *I have learned that there are many things that can make a person sad.*
  • *I have learned that it is good to tell people when you are sad so they can help.*

• Read the book again and look for the vocabulary words.
  • *I see the word **losing** on page 4 and the word **frown** on page 6. The other vocabulary words are found on page 14.*

What makes me **sad**?

Losing makes me sad.

I **frown** when I am sad.

My **friend** moving
away makes me sad.

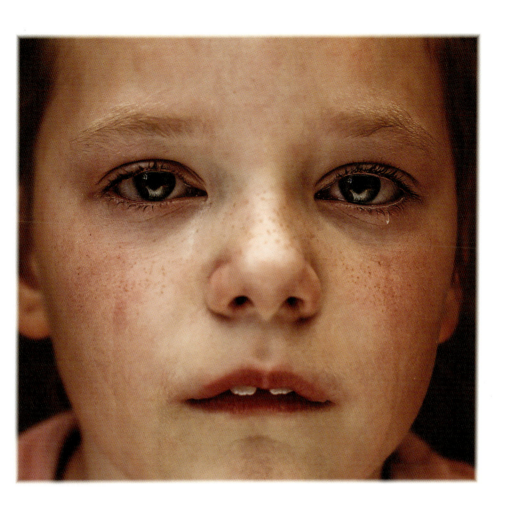

I **cry** when I am sad.

It is good to tell a friend if you are sad.

A friend can help you.

What makes you sad?

Word List
Sight Words

a	makes	what
am	me	when
good	my	you
I	to	

Words to Know

cry

friend

frown

losing

sad

47 Words

What makes me **sad**?

Losing makes me sad.

I **frown** when I am sad.

My **friend** moving away makes me sad.

I **cry** when I am sad.

It is good to tell a friend if you are sad.

A friend can help you.

What makes you sad?

CRABTREE
Publishing Company

Written by: Amy Culliford

Designed by: Rhea Wallace

Series Development: James Earley

Proofreader: Ellen Rodger

Educational Consultant: Marie Lemke M.Ed.

Photographs:
Shutterstock: Juan Pablo Gonzaález: cover; Eveny
    Atamanenko: p. 1; icsnaps: p. 3, 14; Brocreative: p. 5,
    14; Evgenyrychko: p. 7, 14; TTstock: p. 8, 14; Matryoha:
    p. 9, 14; szefei: p. 10-11; wavebreakmedia: p. 13

My Emotions
SAD

Library and Archives Canada Cataloguing in Publication

Title: Sad / Amy Culliford.
Names: Culliford, Amy, 1992- author.
Description: Series statement: My emotions |
    "A Crabtree roots book".
Identifiers: Canadiana (print) 20210156600 |
    Canadiana (ebook) 20210156619 |
    ISBN 9781427139665 (hardcover) |
    ISBN 9781427139726 (softcover) |
    ISBN 9781427133373 (HTML) |
    ISBN 9781427139788 (read-along ebook) |
    ISBN 9781427133977 (EPUB)
Subjects: LCSH: Sadness in children—Juvenile literature. |
    LCSH: Sadness—Juvenile literature.
Classification: LCC BF723.S15 C85 2021 | DDC j152.4—dc23

Library of Congress Cataloging-in-Publication Data

Available at the Library of Congress

Crabtree Publishing Company

www.crabtreebooks.com   1-800-387-7650

Printed in the U.S.A./062021/CG20210401

Published in the United States
Crabtree Publishing
347 Fifth Avenue, Suite 1402-145
New York, NY, 10016

Published in Canada
Crabtree Publishing
616 Welland Ave.
St. Catharines, Ontario L2M 5V6